T0095515

Hostages on the SUBWAY

Wendy Elmer

authorHOUSE®

AuthorHouse™
1663 Liberty Drive
Bloomington, IN 47403
www.authorhouse.com
Phone: 1-800-839-8640

Published by AuthorHouse 6/17/2013

ISBN: 978-1-4817-6627-2 (sc)
ISBN: 978-1-4817-6626-5 (e)

CHAPTER 1

In the year of our Lord 1990 the then governor of Nevada found money in his budget to build the first subway in Las Vegas. He let the word out and so many people showed up to apply for jobs that they had to shut down the procedure until the next day. Many people were rejected because of not having the right licenses. The plan was to run it from each of the casinos on the strip to as far as the hospital. This would make it easier to get from one casino to the other without overburdening the bus situation. It was also hoped that the commuters who live in the city and work on the strip would be eased of the overcrowding problem. The carfare was set at a dollar one way. Remarkably the project was finished within one year. On opening day there was a huge ribbon cutting ceremony. All of the casinos had a medical doctor and nurse on call for minor problems. In cases of a heart attack or cancer treatment side effects the hospital was called to send an ambulance. The most common medical problem was the customers couldn't pee and had to be catheterized. People would sit and gamble for hours on end and then couldn't make when they finally gave in. During the construction of the subway the state of Nevada had the distinction of having the lowest unemployment rate in the country. They also had a population explosion because they were only hiring current residents for the jobs. When the subway was finished there was a mass exodus from the construction workers.

CHAPTER 2

Detective Schapiro and his wife Joyce were walking their dog in the park when Joyce decided to get together with Ronald and Eloise Dennelly. They had become fast friends over the past two years. Joyce made the phone call right away and Ronald agreed to it right away. They decided to meet in the diner for breakfast and take it from there. Robert had special privelages to bring his dog Daisy into the supermarket. Daisy helped out with a Code Adam about two months previously. She successfully found a child in the cookie aisle. Robert brought the dog into the supermarket quite by accident. He just walked in and forgot the dog was with him. Everybody loved the Beagle. She adored all the attention. When this happened the staff immediately found Robert and Robert took over the case. They all went into the supermarket and went straight for the lunch meat counter. Joyce was in charge of the food. She brought a pound of ham, a pound of spiced ham, a pound of macaroni salad, and a pound of potato salad.

Robert saw that and asked: "Who are you feeding and army? With all that food you can invite my whole squad to join you."

Joyce said: "You and Ronald can put it away like nobody's business and you know it."

Robert said: "Ronald doesn't eat like that anymore. He is off his insulin and eats much different now."

Joyce said: "Blah, blah, blah!!! I will feed your squad lunch with the leftovers. Eloise and I have to eat too you know. What do you think we are going to do sit there and knit a sweater while you guys stuff your faces?"

Robert said: "Don't forget the soda and cups. Ronald likes Diet Pepsi."

Joyce went off and brought a box of 12 cans of Diet Pepsi. The dog Daisy got a treat of snacks and then they went off to the lines to pay for their groceries.

CHAPTER 3

The next day everybody met at Robert's house and trouped over to the diner for breakfast. They ere always welcome in the diner. All the workers knew the group. They could never bring Daisy into the restaurant because of the health code. There was a rumor going around that an undercover inspector was in the area. Two diners already lost their licenses because of violations. Robert gave a tip to get the waitresses to clean the colored nail polish from their fingers. Itr was always a pleasure to serve Ronald and Eloise because their daughter was remarkably well behaved. For a two year old there were no meltdowns or throwing of food. Joyce asked them about that once. Eloise said they keep her calm by playing tapes of classical music right around bed time. She sleeps all night. There were only a few sleepless nights when she was teething. Once they popped through she settled down. They were very blessed to have a happy baby.

5

About half was through the meal Robert got a phone call that there was an emergency meeting with Norman the Commissioner. As expected he had to leave right away,. He said his good byes and walked out the door.

CHAPTER 4

The rest of the group started discussing their plans for the picnic. That was a mistake because the two people sitting in the booth behind them were criminals. Abraham and Aaron overheard that Robert was a police sergeant. They started formulating a plan for a crime. They stayed and had another cup of coffee each. They also had a slice of apple pie and a custard cake slice. By the time Abraham finished his pie he had the whole idea hatched.

Abraham said: "Follow my lead Aaron. Just do exactly what I say."

When Robert's group left Abraham and Aaron followed about ten feet behind. They followed the group, but they never noticed. Ronald, Eloise, and Joyce were too busy discussing their day ahead. They all made it to the first stop on the subway and boarded with the rest of the crowd. Eloise carried the diaper bag and Ronald carried Arlene. Then

Joyce carried the picnic basket. They decided to leave the stroller at home. There was no room on the subway. The overcrowding problem was never really solved. Everybody paid their dollar and boarded the train. Between the Venetian and Imperial hotels the two thugs made their move. Abraham pulled the emergency cord. Everybody went flying all over the place. There were no serious injuries yet. Just bumps and bruises.

The conductor's name was Peter. He had to leave his booth and walk through the train to find the source of the stallment. He yelled: "Is everybody all right? Are there any injuries?"

Everybody said: "No sir!! No injuries over here!!!"

Peter had to get out of the train and walk the track to see what the problem was.

He yelled: "Ladies and gentlemen. I have to walk the track and see what the problem is. I will be right back. Please just relax and let me take care of it. The conductor Mark can assist you in anything you need."

CHAPTER 5

At this point Abraham finally made his move. Aaron shot out a gun shot into the ceiling. That got everyone's attention. Everyone was shepherded into the next car. Ronald, Eloise, and Joyce and Arlene were left inside the car. The conductor came running in to see what was the commotion.

Abraham told Joyce to call her husband right away. She got him on the phone and gave the phone to Abraham. He said: "Listen Robert. I have a bomb on board the subway. It is under the train car that your wife is in. You will do as I say or I will blow up your wife and all the subway with them. Stand back and await further instructions." Robert was rather puzzled and upset about this phone call. He sought advice from Norman the Commissioner.

Norman said: "You are personally involved in the case. You are not allowed to get involved or work this case at all. Is that clear?"

Robert said: "Yes sir. I understand. What should I do?"

Norman asked: "What did the caller say?"

Robert said: "The voice told me to stand by and await further instructions."

Norman said: "Then that is what you will do. Your wife's life is on the line. Also the lives of your friends the Dennelly's. Don't do anything to risk their lives. In the mean time we will send half the police force down there."

Robert said: "The guy said no cops. I can't risk any lives."

Norman said: "Relax. The people going in there are plain clothes cops. They don't look any different than any other tourist. Their badges and guns are hiding.

CHAPTER 6

Nobody noticed this but Ronald was texting Robert the whole time keeping him apprised of the situation. He texted that their names were Aaron and Abraham. This was crucial information for Norman.

Norman pulled Robert aside and asked: "Have you ever put anybody in jail for crimes with these names?"

Robert said: "I don't know. Once they are found guilty I dismiss them from my mind."

Norman said: "Go through your files and look. Start with the A's. Somebody told me your files are alphabetized by the perpetrator's name. The cabinets are in the office next to yours."

Robert said: "Wait a second sir. Abraham and Aaron are first names. Our files are alphabetized by last names."

James interrupted and said: "Excuse me sir. I can work with Robert to get him focused."

Norman said: "Thank you James. Get to work."

James and Robert opened the top drawer of the filing cabinet in the next room.

James said: "Look at the first names on each folder. Find one that says Abraham or Aaron."

Robert found one that said Abramovich, Aaron. Robert looked on the last page and found his signature on it. That indicated that this defendant was a case that Robert worked and closed. James found one folder that said Hertzberg, Abraham. He pulled the two folders and brought them to Norman in the next room. He said: "Norman, we found the defendants." James ran in the next room and told Norman that they possibly have the full names of the perpetrators.

Norman said: "Robert, send a text to Ronald and ask if their last names are Hertzberg and Abramovich."

About fifteen minutes later Robert found out that they had the names of all the parties involved. Norman instructed Robert to sit down and not to move. He was taken to an interrogation room with four uniformed officers guarding him.

Norman said to the officers that Robert was not to get out of the chair for any reason. If he moves shoot him. Don't sneeze, fart, cough, or belch for any reason."

Now that Robert was confined to a room the rest of the cops got to work.

CHAPTER 7

I n the situation room beneath them there gathered the former governor and the supervisor of the track layers. They dug up the original blueprints for the work to be done. They were drove in by the cops with lights and sirens blaring. The four of them identified the possible spots where a bomb might be planted. The conductor already shut off the electricity so that the train couldn't move. Ronald texted Robert and kept him informed of all the updates. The uniformed cops called out the information on the radio to Norman. They all breathed a sigh of relief when they heard that.

CHAPTER 8

The hostage negotiation team arrived at the train station. One person was in charge of the negotiations. It was his job to end the situation peacefully and without injury. The leader was named Marvin McCallister.

Marvin walked the tracks with his team of nine other people. They spread themselves out at regular intervals. Marvin took the megaphone and said: "Abraham, what seems to be the trouble today?"

Abraham said: "I am taking hostages."

Marvin asked: "Why?"

Abraham said: "What kind of question is that?"

Marvin said: "Most people who take hostages want something in return."

Abraham said: "What I want nobody can give back to me. I was convicted and jailed for five years for armed robbery. Joyce's husband Robert Schapiro is the one who put me in jail. I want my five years back."

Marvin asked: "How did you recognize Joyce as Robert's wife?"

Abraham said: "I recognized Robert in the diner this morning. They were stupid enough to talk about their day and where they will be today in public. All I did was eavesdrop on their conversation. The last time I checked eavesdropping wasn't a crime."

Marvin asked: "How would this change your past?"

Abraham said: "I don't know I can't get my life back. Five years that I lost."

Marvin asked: "What can we do to help you solve this problem?"

Abraham said: "I have a problem. I don't know how to end this. I really don't want to kill anybody. Robert has to understand that he can't steal people's lives and not get revenge."

Marvin said: "Joyce and Ronald are both diabetic. How about you let the hostages go just so they can eat?"

Abraham said: "I don't want to go back to jail."

Marvin said: "That is not up to me. My job is to keep them safe and to get you some help."

Abraham said: "Oh all right. Get them out of here."

They were released after two hours of negotiations unharmed. They were taken by ambulance to the Las Vegas hospital for observation. Robert picked them up in a police car and took full responsibility for their safe keeping. He signed his signature so many times that day on so many forms he forgot how to spell his name literally. Abraham and Aaron was arrested on the spot.]'"

CHAPTER 9

The next day Robert was woken up by the phone. He was called back to the scene of the crime. At 3:00 a.m. the bomb went off and blew up the rail. The clock was programmed incorrectly as 3:00 a.m. instead of 3:00 p.m. The electricity was turned back on after it was determined that there was no bomb. It was hiding very cleverly. There were no injuries because nobody was on the train in the first car. That was pure luck because the doors were not functioning properly. There were maybe ten people on the train at once. Most of them were too high or drunk to notice. One person thought it was a freak thunderstorm. He sobered up immediately. When the cops saw the state they were in they were driven to the hotel rooms and put to bed. They all promised to stay in the hotel room until they were sober. Surprisingly nobody broke that promise. The cops visited them the next morning and took down their information. They all agreed to come back to testify against the bomb planters. Everybody showed up at the trial. It was explained to them that the cops from the Las Vegas police department takes the role of educating the public, not necessarily arresting everybody they run in to. They do run into kids who come there to get stupid. They have to act like parents sometimes. These witnesses were so impressed that they relocated to Las Vegas within a year. They felt safe there knowing the police were going to protect them.

CHAPTER 10

Abraham and Aaron were accused of planting a bomb on the subway and causing bodily harm. A grand jury came back with a verdict that they had enough evidence to proceed to trial. One at a time they were brought before a judge. Judge Samuels said: "First case on the docket is the case against Abraham Hertzberg. People on bail?"

The lawyer for the people said: "Louise Johnson for the people your honor. People request remand and held over for trial."

Judge Samuels said: "Defense attorney?"

The defense said: "Martha Jackson for the defense your honor. We request R.O.R. for both defendants."

Judge Samuels said; "I only see one defendant before me. Where is the other one?"

Martha said: "I am also the defense attorney for the second defendant Aaron Abramovitch."

Judge Samuels said: "Bring in Aaron."

The court officers brought Aaron and Abraham up to the desk just as they were told they were being held over for trial. Judge Samuels ordered that the two of them share a cell to come up with a story as to why they engaged in this heinous act.

CHAPTER 11

The food in the jail wasn't half bad. They were fed in their cells so that they weren't rushed. They didn't run the risk of being shanked. For dinner they had mashed potatoes, peas, and roast beef. The gravy dripped all over their clothes. It was heavenly because they couldn't eat like that on the outside. To drink they each had a can of coke. Hot water wasn't allowed because the officials were afraid somebody would have a meltdown and throw hot water in someone's face.

Abraham asked: "So let's get started. What do you think will be our punishment?"

Aaron said: "This is your third strike, so probably you will get life."

Abraham said: "I did most of the work. You just had to stand there and make sure nothing went wrong. I think the judge will go easy on you."

Aaron said: "Everybody knows the what of what

we did. What about the why of what happened? What are we going to tell the judge about that?"

Abraham said: "I was just angry at the world. I couldn't help myself. I had five years to build it up. When I saw Detective Schapiro at the diner I could barely contain myself. It all came bubbling up again. I had to get revenge. I blame Detective Schapiro because it was his testimony that got me there."

Aaron asked: "Did you want a ransom?"

Abraham said: "Yes. I wanted an enormous amount of money. I am having trouble starting my life over."

Aaron asked: "What about the bomb that went off?"

Abraham said: "That was your own foolish fault. You set it up for 3:00 a.m. instead of 3:00 p.m."

Abraham asked: "By the way. What happened to all the other passengers on the train?"

Aaron said: "They were shooed away out the back door. The electricity was cut off so that the passengers can walk safely to the stop behind where we were."

Abraham asked: "What does that mean?"

Aaron said: "We were between the Flamingo stop an the Venetian stop. Everybody was exited to the Venetian station."

Abraham asked: "Was anybody electrocuted?"

Aaron said: "No. I just said the electricity was turned off. That is why we all started sweating like we did. No air conditioning."

Abraham asked: If you were in the car with me how do you know all this?"

Aaron said: "I watched out the window."

CHAPTER 12

Detective Schapiro received a phone call from Mary Kelly. She was the warden of the local jail. She offered her services for consultation on these two ex prisoners. She set up a meeting with Robert and the squad the next day. Robert would do anything for a free cup of coffee and a donut. Mary always made sure he got a decaf. Mary always had to have her nerves intact, so she rarely drank coffee on the job.

The squad arrived thirty minutes early so they ha time to go through all the metal detectors and be buzzed in. Mary assigned one of the officers to escort them through so they don't get lost.

Robert opened with: "So Mary. How are the prisoners? Are they giving you any trouble?"

Mary said: " Some of them do. The lifers are giving me the least trouble. They get the priveledge of doing a Scared Straight episode. That earns them an extra hour outside of their cells. I watched them through the closed circuit TV screens. They know enough not to physically touch the kids."

Robert asked: "What is that shouting?"

Mary said: "That is the boot camp training. They parade around the grounds learning to walk properly. in the end their families are invited to share in the graduation. We get a lot of thank yous from the prisoners. They also are expected to make their beds every morning. The graduates of this program take the new prisoners under their wing to adjust to prison life. Nobody knows this but these graduates average about six months early release. Our oldest graduate is 59 years old female. We also have a 59 year old male. They call themselves the grandparents of the program. They are actually the grandparents of the whole jail. These prisoners who finish the program have a two percent return rate. The grandparents are both lifers, but they are given cells that are slightly bigger. I use John as an example of our success. I never use his last name or where he works."

John said: "I appreciate that Mary . I don't need anyone following me."

Mary asked: "So Robert. How is Ronald doing these day?"

Robert said: "He is doing fine. They have a two year old daughter now."

Mary said: "Wonderful!!! I didn't know they had another baby!!!"

Robert said: "Actually she was adopted. The baby fell into my life by a teenage mother. She left her at the precinct under the baby safe haven law. Naturally I thought of Ronald and Eloise. Ronald almost fell over when I showed up at the door with a baby. They took the baby without thinking twice. This happened about a year after they lost their first daughter."

Mary said: "I heard Ronald and Eloise were caught up in the subway caper."

Robert said: "Yes. They were all hospitalized overnight for observation. When they were released I signed my name so many times I forgot how to spell it."

John said: "Excuse me Mary. I was just thinking. I don't remember those two grandparents here."

Mary said: "They are lifers, so you were never exposed to them. You were housed in a different unit than they are. You also didn't take in any new prisoners under your wing and show them the ropes of prison life."

Robert said: So Mary. Please tell us about those two bozos."

Mary said: "As usual we have on leader and one follower. Abraham in this case was the leader. Aaron was the follower."

Robert asked: "Were they troublemakers here?"

Mary said: "Abraham had anger issues. He was angry at you for taking away his life for five years. You were lucky he didn't come after you personally."

Robert said: "Actually he did. Except he came after my wife instead of me personally."

They all said their good byes and Mary called for two guards to escort them off the premesis. Mary promised to testify in case she is needed.

CHAPTER 13

The judge in this case decided not to throw them back in jail. They wore an ankle monitor to keep them in the house. Their TV, computers, laptops, and telephones were all removed. All they could do was stare at the four walls. If they tried to leave the apartment an alarm would sound in the sheriff's office and an APB would go out immediately. They had virtually no contact with the outside world. They looked out the window and found a 24 hour guard outside their building. Aaron had to stand by the window to hold up a sign and ask for food. It was called in to the judge. The cops forgot to fill in the refrigerator. Another cop car came by and the two officers went out to the store with a shopping list. They came back with milk, bread, eggs, butter, crackers, and a few other snacks. Abraham practically lost his mind without a TV and a connection to the outside world. Aaron told him to get used to it. He has done it before and he can do it again. Abraham almost stabbed him to death. The cops had to burst down the door when neighbors heard yelling. They feared the roommate might be in danger. When they broke down the door Abraham was sitting on top of Aaron with a plastic knife pointed at Aaron's jugular vein. He was pummeling him to a pulp. His face was all bruised and his nose was all bloodied. Abraham was removed to the squad car and had a spit guard put on his face. He was driven to the detention center and strapped to a gurney. Aaron had the two other cops sitting with him and cleaning up his face. He went to bed early and didn't give anybody any trouble. Aaron was glad to have a civilized companion to talk to.

CHAPTER 14

The judge was informed about the fight and was not happy about it. She ordered Abraham to stay in the detention center until further notice. A jury selection process was scheduled to start in one week. Abraham was not to be released until then. They looked for a pool of twelve jurors. They had to call twenty four jurors to pick twelve and four alternates. The first person called didn't want to do this, but agreed as an alternate. She was reassured once she was told the defendant would be in jail for the duration of the trial. Three more people were dismissed and everybody else was returned to the jury room. The judge instructed the jury to return on Monday morning by 9:00 a.m. read for the start of the trial. Lateness would not be tolerated. She also informed the jury that interruptions would not be tolerated either. They were to sit quietly and listen.

CHAPTER 15

The first day of the trial of Abraham Hertzberg started like nay other. He showed up at 9:00 a.m. and said good morning to everybody. He wasn't afraid of this trial because it was a non violent case. He expected it to be a short one. He didn't like long trials. Nobody realized this but the judge's job was to make sure the trial ran smoothly. The lawyers had to promise to act like civilized human beings. No interruptions were going to be tolerated.

At precisely 9:00 the jurors picked were called in to the courtroom. The judge said: "Good morning ladies and gentlemen of the jury. My name is Irving Macciaveli. I am the judge in this case. My job is to make sure the lawyers ask questions only relevant to the case at hand. You will not hear ridiculous questions about what his science grades were in the third grade. This case will not last more than two weeks if even that long. On Friday we will leave at 1:00 to give you time to go to your jobs and fill in your time sheets. Despite popular opinion we do have a sensitive side. With that being said James you may begin with your opening statements."

James said: " My name is James Irwin. I am the prosecuting attorney. My job is to prove to you that Abraham is guilty of the crime of planting a bomb and taking hostages on the subway. Our witnesses will prove my point. Thank you."

The judge said: "Melvin, start your opening statement please."

Melvin said: "Than you your honor. My name is Melvin Kotter. I am the defense attorney. You will hear me refer to him as my client. That happens to be Abraham I am talking about. We have come up with a story as to why they did this. We are confident that you will find him not guilty of these crimes."

The judge said: "Thank you Melvin. James, call your first witness please."

James said; "I call Robert Schapiro to the stand." As Robert approached the stand he was sworn in as the fist witness.

James said: "Now Robert. Please tell us about how you got involved in this case."

Robert said: "I was in the diner having breakfast with some friends we were planning a picnic lunch.

As usual O was called away unexpectedly. I left my friend and wife to go to work."

James asked: "Was it a meeting or something?"

Robert said: "Yes. It was a meeting with Norman, our chief of police. I left my wife and friends to have a picnic. I don't know what they talked about after I left."

James asked: "How did you find out there was a problem with your wife?"

Robert said: "She called me and interrupted during a meeting."

James asked: "What was your reaction when you heard?"

Robert said: "Norman is a friend of mine as well as my boss. If anything happense to family he is right there to solve the situation."

James asked: "How did you know who was involved?"

Robert said: "Her cell phone number came up on the caller ID. That is how I knew it was her. I knew it was a dire emergency because she is instructed not to call me unless the house is on fire."

James asked: "Does she always do what you tell her?"

Robert said: "We were married in the church. We

are both religious. Our marriage vows say to love, honor, and obey. We both take that very seriously."

James asked: "What did Norman tell you about getting a phone call?"

Robert said: "We both knew it was an emergency. He said to just answer it."

James said; "No more questions your honor."

The judge said: "Melvin, do you have any questions for this witness?"

Melvin said: "I do your honor. Now Robert, when was your first time meeting Abraham in person?"

Robert said: I first met the defendant about six years ago. According to his file I put him in jail for five years. I have no recollection of his exact crime or anything like that. I just saw my signature on the back of his file."

Melvin asked: "What about for this case?"

Robert said; "Oh. It was this morning."

Melvin asked: "How do you indict a person without ever meeting him?"

Robert said: "It was the text messages that I read. It was also the grand jury that indicted him, not me."

Melvin said; "Thank you Robert. No more questions your honor."

The judge said: " Thank you Robert. No more questions your honor."

The judge said: "You may step down Robert. Due to the time we will adjourn for lunch. Everybody return her in one hour for the afternoon session."

CHAPTER 16

Everybody returned in one hour just as instructed The judge said: "James, call your next witness please."

James said: "I call Fred O'Connor to the stand." As Fred approached the stand he was sworn in by the bailiff."

James asked: "How did you become involved in this case?"

Fred said: "I was there when the explosion happened. The cop interviewed me and I was so impressed that I relocated here to Las Vegas. He said sometimes the cops had to act like parents because people come here to get stupid. The cops spend some time being substitute parents."

James asked: " Were you drunk at the time?"

Fred said: "Yes. When I heard the big boom I thought it was thunder. I sobered right up."

James said: "No more questions your honor."

The judge said: "Melvin, do you have any questions for this witness?"

Melvin said: "I do your honor. Now Fred, did you personally see my client plant the bomb?"

Fred said: "No sir. I did not."

Melvin asked: "How can you testify against my client then?"

Fred said: "I am not sure if I am testifying against him, but I am just here to tell what happened. I relocated here because the cops treated me with respect even though I was stupidly drunk. I pretended to be sober."

Melvin asked: "Were you arrested that night?"

Fred said: "No. I remember somebody escorted me back to my hotel room and I promised not to leave until I was completely sober. I kept that promise. I remember not eating much because my stomach was upset. Since I was just 18 years old I wasn't accustomed to drinking and didn't know what a hangover felt like. I can assure you I haven't taken a drink ever since. I have taken up a cause since I moved here. Last week I got permission from the local high school principal to take an afternoon of a seminar about the after effects of drinking and getting drunk. He allowed me to talk to the whole school. I never had a course in the after effects. I was hoping to reach young kids."

Melvin said: "Thank you Fred. No more questions your honor."

The judge said; "You may step down Fred. Thank you for your testimony. We will adjourn for the day. Everybody return here tomorrow by 9:00. Have a good evening folks."

CHAPTER 17

At precisely 9:00 the judge entered the courtroom. He said good morning to everybody. Day 2 started out simple enough. The judge said: "James, call your first witness please."

James said: "I call Joyce Schapiro to the stand." As Joyce approached the stand she was sworn in as a witness. She took her seat.

James asked: "Joyce, how did you become involved in this case?"

Joyce said: "I was one of the hostages taken."

James asked: "How were you picked as a victim for this caper?"

Joyce said: "I don't think I now for sure. Maybe it was wrong place wrong time."

James asked; "Do you blame yourself for this danger you were in with Ronald and Eloise?"

Joyce said: "Not at all. We were all together and we got through it. We protected each other."

James said: "No more questions your honor."

The judge said: "Melvin, do you have any questions for this witness?"

Melvin said: "Yes your honor. Now Joyce, when was the first time you met the defendant?"

Joyce said: "The day we did the picnic was the first time we met."

Melvin asked: "Was this on the subway or at the diner?"

Joyce said: "This was on the subway. When he took us as hostages. He pointed us out and his partner shoved everybody else into the next car."

Melvin asked: "Did you talk directly to him?"

Joyce said: "I don't remember."

Melvin said: "No more questions your honor."

The judge said: "You may step down Joyce. We will adjourn for lunch. Everybody return here in one hour for the afternoon session. Just come straight back here. Have a good lunch."

CHAPTER 18

After an hour everybody returned to the courtroom just as instructed. The judge asked: "James, who is your next witness?"

James said: "I call Marvin McCallister to the stand." As Marvin approached the stand he was sworn in as a witness. He took his seat.

James asked: "Marvin, please tell us how you got involved in this case."

Marvin said: "I was assigned to the hostage negotiation team for the day."

James asked: How often do you change your assignment?"

Marvin said: "We change everyday. This way people don't get a chance to study the styles of different negotiators."

James asked: "Did you get any special training for this?"

Marvin said: "Yes. This was special schooling after I was instructed as a cop. Just because you graduate doesn't mean you automatically go out on street patrol. Some people are assigned to the detention center or the jail. The detention center and the jail are considered cushy jobs because we are not out on the street. We are not out there exposed to the desert heat."

James asked: "What else is changed all the time?"

Marvin said: "Anybody who does school patrol we have a different color for the day. This question comes out just in case anybody pretends to be a cop and turns out the be a sex offender. We have a computer at our disposal to check any name. With our computers we can look up just about anything except their breakfast foods. I can look up your name and tell you more about yourself than you even knew."

The judge interrupted and said: "Hold on there Marvin. I would like to put you to the test on that. Look up my name tonight on your computer and tell me everything about me."

Marvin said: "I will take you up on that. All I need is your name."

The judge said: "Report to my office tomorrow morning at 8:00. Bring me everything you have. If you come up with more information than I would like to let out then I will eat my hat. You are dismissed."

Marvin said: "Please write down your name on a piece of paper." He did so and Marvin left the court house and got straight to work.

The judge said: "Everybody is dismissed for the evening. Please return here by 9:00 tomorrow morning. Have a good evening everybody. With that I bid you all a good day. Lawyers please report to my office by 8:00 tomorrow morning with plans for the day." With that everybody went home.

CHAPTER 19

At precisely 8:00 the next morning the lawyers met the judge outside his chambers. They had to wait for the arrival of two bailiffs. Whenever he talked to the lawyers he always wanted witnesses to his words. The judge looked forward to these meetings because it was his chance to smile and act human. The bailiffs arrived within 5 minutes and apologized for their tardiness. The judge forgave them for their transgressions. He invited them to sit down. He said: "So. How do you think the trial is going?"

Both lawyers said: "Fine sir. Thank you sir."

The judge said: "This is day 3 of the trial and so far you haven't said much in the way of defense."

The defense attorney said: "That will change today sir."

The judge said: "Let's see if we can direct this show to look like a trial."

Both lawyers agreed to this plan. With that

there was a knock on the door and Marvin was let in. He came in about 8:20 with the information the judge requested. He came back with his name, his wife's name, his wife's maiden name and the names of all of his kids. He looked up the judge's last three addresses. He also came up with the names of his three kids. Marvin did an advanced search and came up with the judge's bank balances. He almost fell off the chair when he saw that. The judge asked: "Did you get this information from the computer in your car?"

Marvin said: "Not all of it. Some I went into the computer at home. Nowadays you can get information about everything. Your toilet deposits didn't show up. Forgive me for being so personal. That wasn't my intent."

The judge said: "Let's call the court to order shall we?"

Everybody went into the court room and the judge was glad to see everybody was there. He said good morning to the jury. Then he said: "Melvin, I believe Marvin was at the witness stand last. Do you have any questions for this witness?"

Melvin said: "No sir. I do not."

The judge said: "Very well. You may step down Marvin. And by the way. All that research you did last night won't ever leave your lips. Shred everything and forget you ever saw it. Is that clear?"

Marvin said: "Yes sir. Absolutely. Without a doubt."

CHAPTER 20

The judge said: "James, do you have anymore witnesses?"

James said: "No sir. The prosecution rests your honor."

The judge said: "Very well. Melvin, you may call your first witness please."

Melvin said: "I call Abraham Hertzberg to the stand." As Abraham approached he was sworn in as the witness. He took his seat.

The judge said: "Please state your name for the record."

Abraham said: "My names is Abraham Hertzberg."

Melvin asked: "Were you the perpetrator of this crime?"

Abraham said: "Yes sir. I took hostages on the subway."

Melvin asked: "What about the bombing of the subway car?"

Abraham said: "That was my partner. The stupid fool set it for 3:00 a.m. instead of 3:00 p.m."

Melvin asked: "Did you know the people you took as hostages?"

Abraham said: "Not personally no. But they were picked by me personally."

Melvin asked: "How did you happen to pick them personally?"

Abraham said: "I saw Robert at the diner in the next booth. The other two people I didn't know. I remembered Robert as being the cop responsible for putting me in jail for five years. I wanted my life back. I eavesdropped on their conversation and found out their plans for the day. Last I heard eavesdropping wasn't a crime. I just followed them. The dumb idiots didn't even notice me behind them."

Melvin asked: "What were you trying to prove by taking them hostage?"

Abraham said: "I don't know. I was just so angry with Robert I guess I didn't think it through."

Melvin asked: "Was this your first experience taking hostages?"

Abraham said: "Yes. How did you know?"

Melvin said: "Because Ronald was texting Robert the whole time. That tells me you aren't very observant."

Abraham lost his temper and screamed: "Now you just wait a cotton picking minute genius. Watching them was the job of my partner Aaron. He never could get anything right the little imp. You tell him to pee and he'll ask where to aim it. I should have known better than to trust an idiot like that!!!"

Melvin asked: "When did he plant the bomb?"

Abraham said: "During the day. He was fast about it. The subway runs only once every half hour. He waited for the train to pass and then jumped onto the track to plant it. He was very quick about it. Maybe that is why he screwed up."

Melvin asked: "Isn't the electricity turned off?"

Abraham said: "No sir. The electricity is kept on all day. It is only turned off at 4:00 a.m. when the last train has left the station. They turn it off for two hours to do track maintenance."

Melvin said: "This tells me you have done some research before on it."

Abraham said: "My father worked on the building of the subway. That is how I know all the details."

Melvin said: "According to records you and Aaron were rejected from building the subway. Is that accurate?"

Abraham said: "Yes. I hadn't earned an electrical license at the time."

Melvin said: "No more questions your honor."

The judge said: "James, do you have any questions for this witness?"

James said: "I do your honor. Now Abraham, please tell us about the fight you had with Aaron the week before this trial."

Melvin said: "OBJECTION YOUR HONOR!!! He is not on trial for the fight.!!"

The judge said: "OVERRULED!! I'll allow it. But James, I am warning you. You had better show relevance here."

James said: "I will your honor. Abraham, why did that happen?"

Abraham said: "I was going crazy because they took away my TV, internet, phone, and they virtually cut us off from the outside world. I needed to have humanity."

James asked: "You had Aaron, wasn't that enough?"

Abraham said: "They didn't give us any food. He had to hold a sign out the window to get them to give us something. That was inhumane and I cracked under the pressure. I just took it out on Aaron."

James said: "No more questions your honor."

The judge said: "Very well James. Everybody will break for lunch and when we return in one hour we will hear closing arguments from both sides. You are al dismissed because I am starving."

CHAPTER 21

An hour later everybody was seated and ready to proceed with the next phase of the trial. The judge said: "Good afternoon ladies and gentlemen. The lawyers will now give their arguments. After that I will give you instructions on deliberations. For now just concentrate on the closing arguments. James will go first because he is the prosecuting attorney. Take it away James."

James got up and said; "Thank you your honor. Ladies and gentlemen of the jury. As the prosecuting attorney I was supposed to prove that the defendant did it. He even admitted it. You must find the defendant guilty of the charge of hostage taking. That is his only charge. Thank you."

With that Melvin got up and said: "Ladies and gentlemen of the jury. I was the defense attorney in this case. He had no intention of causing harm to the hostages. He just wanted to get revenge for what

Robert did. You must find my client not guilty of this crime. Thank you."

The judge said: "Ladies and gentlemen of the jury. You have heard both sides of the argument. You will deliberate until 3:00. That give you one hour. You will communicate with me through the guard. Send me a note if you need any read backs. The lawyers will be in my office in the meantime. Bailiff, escort these jurors to the room please."

With that they all adjourned.

CHAPTER 22

They sat around for ten minutes and had coffee and cookies for a snack. Then they started to talk about the case. Everybody had their own opinion but they pretty much agreed he was guilty. It had to be 12 out of 12 jurors. They sent a note through the guard that they have reached a verdict. The lawyers were nervous because it came back too quickly. They reassembled in the jury room. They bailiff yelled: "ALL RISE!!" and the judge entered the courtroom.

The judge asked: "Has the jury reached a verdict?"

The foreman said: "We have your honor. We find the defendant guilty of taking hostages. We find the defendant not guilty of the charge of planting a bomb."

The judge said: "Abraham, I sentence you to 15 years in state prison for taking hostages. Ladies and gentlemen of the jury. Thank you for your service.

You may return to the jury room for dismissal after you get your papers."

The defendant was led away in handcuffs and returned to state prison. His face practically burned people with anger.

CHAPTER 23

The trial for Aaron Abramovitch was scheduled to start on September 1st. The judge in this case was named Joshua Foley. The prosecuting attorney was named Isaac Johnson. The defense attorney was named Harry Purcell. All parties were convened into judge Foley's courtroom at 9:00 the day the trial was to begin. The jury was picked in one morning. Twelve jurors were needed. There was only one person who had to get out of it. She was let go because of a series of strokes. The judge didn't want that kind of excitement in his court.

The judge said: "Tomorrow will be day one of this trial. It should not take longer than a week. The defendant is accused of planting a bomb on the subway. That is the only issue here. You will not hear ridiculous questions no relevant to this case. Everybody come here by 9:00 for the start of the trial. You are excused for the day.

CHAPTER 24

Day 1 of the trial of Aaron started right on time at 9:00 a.m. The jury assembled and the court was called to order. The judge said: "Isaac, please begin with your opening statements."

Isaac said: "Ladies and gentlemen of the jury. My name is Isaac Johnson. I am the prosecuting attorney in this case. My job is to prove that the defendant planted the bomb n the subway. By the end of this trial you must find the defendant guilty of planting the bomb. Thank you.

The judge said: "Harry, you may begin with your opening statements please."

Harry said: "Thank you your honor. My name is Harry Purcell. I am the defense attorney for this case. My job is to prove that Aaron didn't do this. Thank you."

The judge said: "Isaac, call your first witness please."

Isaac said: "I call Robert Schapiro to the stand."

As Robert approached the stand he was sworn in as the witness.

Isaac asked: "So Robert. How did you come about charging the defendant with this crime?"

Robert said: "I received a phone call from my wife that there was a problem on the subway. Ronald sent me a text message telling me his situation. I told him to try and get the last name. I got his last name from the files that James showed me next door. He got me to try and focus on solving the problem at hand. In this case it was to get the person responsible for this interruption on their day. I was not allowed to get personally involved since my wife was in the thick of it. I was trying to find a resolution for someone else to do."

Isaac asked: "Were you there when the bomb went off?"

Robert said: "No sir. The bomb squad was called in and there was enough left of the bomb to get serial numbers. It was made of nails and fluid. When the bomb exploded the nails were supposed to fly all over and stab everyone. If the nails flew in the right direction people wouldn't be stabbed in the chest and head."

Isaac asked: "How many injuries were there at this event?"

Robert said: "I think there was only one or two injuries. The person sitting right on top of the bomb and he was stabbed in the buttocks. The EMS pulled the nail out and gave him a tetanus shot on the scence. He went home. One was stabbed in the chest by a nail. He was taken to the hospital for surgery, but he died on the table. That was the only fatality."

Isaac asked: "Did you personally witness the defendant plant the bomb?"

Robert said: "No sir. I did not."

Isaac asked: "What made you conclude the fact that my defendant did this?"

The judge interrupted and said: "Hold it Isaac. That question has already been answered. That second question will be struck from the record."

Isaac said: "Sorry your honor. Let's try this question. Were you personally there when the bomb went off?"

Robert said: "No sir. I was woken up from a deep sleep when it happened. It happened at 3:00 a.m. instead of 3:00 p.m."

Isaac said: "No more questions your honor."

The judge said: "Harry, do you have any questions for this witness?"

Harry said: "Yes sir. Now Robert, when did you last have any dealing with the defendant?"

Robert said: "According to the police report I arrested him on a charge of robbery. I have no personal memory of the exact case. He was found guilty and was sent to jail. For some reason he blames me for his troubles."

Harry asked: "Did you keep in touch with him after you sent him to jail?"

Robert said: "I did not send him to jail. That was the jury because he was found guilty of the crimes he committed. I did not personally put the gun in his hand. He and he alone did that."

Harry asked: "How did you come about arresting my client and charging him with planting the bomb?"

Robert said: "Ronald and I kept texting each other. Then we read the files of closed cases. We had his home address in the files. He is supposed to register whenever he moves."

Harry asked: "Is he a registered sex offender?"

Robert said: "No. He is supposed to register with his parole officer. He is also supposed to register as a resident in the DMV. He was very easy to find."

Harry asked; "Did you personally witness the defendant planting the bomb?"

Robert said: "No sir. I wasn't there when the bomb went off."

Harry said: "No more questions your honor."

The judge said: "Ladies and gentlemen of the jury. I have a dentist appointment this afternoon. We will adjourn for the day until tomorrow. Use this time wisely and go to your jobs and fill out your timesheets. Everybody return here by 9:00 tomorrow morning by 9:00. Lawyers will meet me in my office at 8:00 in the morning. Have a nice evening everybody."

The bailiff yelled: "ALL RISE!!!" Everybody rose and exited the courtroom.

CHAPTER 25

The lawyers met in the judge's chambers at 8:00 the next morning. They had coffee together. The judge asked: "Whom are you planning to call today?"

The prosecuting attorney said: "We are planning on calling the guy who was in the train at the time of the bombing. We are also planning on calling Ronald. Maybe tomorrow we will call Eloise and Joyce. The defense attorney countered that and said they might call Joyce today depending on time constraints today." With that they all adjourned to the courtroom. The judge put on his serious and straight face. The bailiff yelled "ALL RISE!!!"

Day 2 of the trial started right on time The judge said: "Isaac, call your first witness please."

Isaac said: "I call Ronald Dennelly to the stand." As Ronald approached the stand he was sworn in as a witness.

Isaac said: "Now Ronald. Please tell us about the day of the event."

Ronald said: "Robert has been a friend of ours for about three years now. His wife Joyce planned a picnic for us. We started out with breakfast in our favorite diner. We planned to go to the park on the subway."

Isaac asked: "Did you talk about it out loud?"

Ronald said: "Yes sir. We talked about it during breakfast."

Isaac asked: "Did you have your daughter with you?"

Ronald said: "Yes sir. She is two years old now."

Isaac asked: "Is she your birth daughter?"

The judge said: "Objection Isaac. That is irrelevant to this case. Witness does not have to answer that question.. Isaac, I am warning you. Keep your questions relevant to the case. Even if this child dropped down from space in an egg shell that has nothing to do with the bombing."

Isaac said: "I apologize your honor. I won't make that mistake again."

Isaac asked: "Robert, please continue with your story. How did you ge to the subway?"

Robert said: "After we left the diner we walked to the subway."

Isaac asked: "Did you notice the defendant following you to the subway?"

Robert said: "This is Las Vegas. How many people walk behind you along the strip? How are you supposed to pick out one person as opposed to the others following you? I did notice him, but he didn't stand out for any reason. He looked like just another person."

Isaac asked: "What happened when you got on the subway?"

Robert said: "The train disgorged everybody and then we all entered. The doors closed and we took off. Midway between 2 stops the train stopped for a red light. When the light never changed the conductor had to get out and walk the tracks to see if there was a problem with the train. When the conductor left the train that is when the defendant and the accomplice made their move."

Juror number one said: "Excuse me your honor. We have not heard of an accomplice. Are we going to learn about this other person?"

The judge said: "This other person is not on trial here. We are only concerned with this defendant. We don't want you to be influenced by the other person.

I do not know the outcome of his trial because I was not the judge in that case."

Isaac said: "No more questions your honor."

The judge said: "Harry, do you have any questions for this witness?"

Harry said: "Yes sir. Thank you sir. Ronald, were there any injuries after this bombing?"

Ronald said; "I don't know. It happened at 3:00 in the morning. I rode the subway in the early afternoon."

Harry asked: "How did you communicate with Robert during this crisis?"

Ronald said: "I kept texting him. We went back and forth. He doesn't understand texting yet, so he needed an interpreter to translate for him. As a detective he prefers talking to people face to face."

Harry asked; "What was the reaction of your wife when all this happened?"

Ronald said: "She took her cues from me. I talked her to sit next to me and not make a sound. She pretty much does as she is told. That is how our marriage works. I told her to just relax and try to smile."

Harry asked: "What was the reaction of your daughter?"

Ronald said: "She is only two years old. Luckily

she doesn't understand what was happening. The next day she drew a picture of a gun. Naturally it didn't look like one, but it was a raw image. Ever since the event she has been drawing in black. We think she is angry with what happened, but she doesn't have the words yet."

Harry asked: "What about your diabetes?"

Ronald said; "I have to watch the stress level. I started sweating bullets for a while. I stopped sweating when I was sneaking texts to Robert. I felt better knowing he was going to fix this."

Harry asked: "Were you caught texting?"

Ronald said: "No sir. I was very careful about that. I tried to keep the baby calm during the whole sordid affair."

Harry said: "No more questions your honor."

The judge said: "Isaac, do you have any questions for this witness?"

Isaac said: "Yes your honor. Ronald, what was the reaction of Robert's wife Joyce?"

Ronald said: "I just tried to help her relax. I whispered that I would take care of her. She called Robert and talked to him in short clips. We all knew he would get us out of it."

Isaac asked: "Have you ever met the defendant before?"

Ronald said: "No sir. I have never met him before the day of the incident."

Isaac asked: "If you were in charge of the ladies why didn't you look around you to see who was following you?"

Ronald said: "This is Las Vegas. How many people are walking along the strip?"

Isaac asked: "Why did you announce to the whole world your plans for the day?"

Ronald said: "We were in the diner when we talked. All we did was to check in with each other. If we worried about the next person all the time we would all be mute."

Isaac said: "No more questions your honor."

The judge said: "Very well. You may step down Ronald. Because of the time we will adjourn for the day." With that the bailiff yelled "ALL RISE!!!" Everybody rose and were dismissed from the courtroom.

CHAPTER 26

Day 3 of the trial started right on time at 9:00 a.m. The judge did not have a meeting with the lawyers. The judge said: "Harry, you may call your first witness please."

Harry said: "I call Mary Kelly to the stand." As Mary approached she was sworn in as the next witness. Harry asked: "How did you know the defendant?"

Mary said: "He was a prisoner in my jail. I am the warden."

Harry asked: "What kind of prisoner was the defendant?"

Mary said: "He was a pretty cooperative prisoner. He couldn't believe he ran his life into the ditch. I told him we can help him figure out what went wrong in his life. I set him up with the prison psychiatrist. He talked to him and eagerly cooperated with him. He looked forward to these sessions because he got time out of his cell. While he was in with the psychiatrist the guards searched his cell. The guards searched completely and never had a problem with his cell. He eventually earned special privelages as a reward for his cooperation. Most prisoners can't be reformed if we don't get to the bottom of what went wrong in the first place. People think you should lock up criminals for five years and then let them out. They come out worse than when they went in."

Harry asked: "How long have you been the warden of the local jail?"

Mary said: "About ten years now."

Harry asked: "How many break outs have you had in your jail?"

Mary said: "There was just one break out. Every cop in the United States was on the look out for him. The good detectives apprehended him out of state. It tunred out that he was innocent of all charges. We found the real guilty party and drove the prisoner home to his parent's house."

Harry asked: "What happened to the correct prisoner?"

Mary said: "The correct prisoner was executed."

Harry asked: "What else do you do for the prisoners besides the psychiatrist?"

Mary said: "We also have the boot camp

program. We have a zero percent return rate for graduates of the boot camp program. Because of the overcrowding in the jails we get to release prisoners early if they cooperate. Some of the females have meltdowns and have to be put into isolation or a padded room for their protection. I have received a phone call from my superiors that said that there is a waiting list of prisoners asking for placement in my jail. Every six weeks we graduate another group of people out of the boot camp program. We even have some prisoners asking to be released into the military custody. They know all about the Marines by then."

Harry asked: "Did you ever release prisoners into the military?"

Mary said: "A few of them passed the test and were admitted into the Marines. All I can do is pray for them that they will succeed."

Harry said: "No more questions your honor."

The judge said: "Isaac, do you have any questions for this witness?"

Isaac said: "Yes your honor. What do you do for the female prisoners?"

Mary said: "Their feminine needs are being met. Male guards are not allowed in the building with the female prisoners. The guards communicate with each other through the telephone or walkie talkie. They also wear an alarm on their person. If they feel threatened they just push it and guards will be there within a nanosecond. Two male guards accompany me everywhere. If they must enter the building they are never out of my sight."

Isaac asked: "Do you have drills with this alarm on your person?"

Mary said: "No sir. This way if there really is an emergency the guards will know it is for real. We don't want anybody to confuse the drills from the real thing."

Isaac asked: "What is your rate of female prisoner pregnancies?"

Mary said: "Sometimes they arrive pregnant already. Their prenatal care needs are met. After birth the mothers are housed with the babies and the money to pay for diapers are taken out of their paycheck. All they do is the best they can. They do not take off from work. Sometimes the families bring in diapers."

Isaac asked: "Have you ever had a guard be the father of a prisoner's baby?"

Mary said: "All the guards must submit a DNA sample upon being hired. If a baby is born and we suspect a guard somehow we take the DNA from the baby and compare it to the guards."

Isaac asked: "Has this ever happened that a male guard had sex with a female prisoner?"

Mary said: "Yes. Only once. I demanded that he marry the girl and he was promptly fired on the spot. The baby is with the female prisoner now until she lives out her sentence. On the way out we have a shaming ceremony. Life the military. He broke the rules, so he was marched off the grounds as he passed each guard they turned their back to him. I got the idea from a movie I saw. It has never happened again."

Isaac asked: " What kind of prisoner was the defendant?"

Mary said: "He was a rather confused follower. He didn't know if he should listen to me, the guards or his cell mate. One thing was for sure. He just wanted to get out of there.

Isaac asked: "Did he do the boot camp program?"

Mary said: "Yes. He excelled in it."

Isaac asked: "Did he do any other program?

Mary said: "Yes. He was given a job in the library. He picked up a love of reading from there. He already had a high school diploma, so he didn't need that program. He would do anything to be out of his cell."

Isaac said: "No more questions your honor."

The judge said: "Very well. You may step down Mary. Thank you for your testimony." With that Mary stepped down and left the courthouse. She had to return to the jail for the rest of the day.

The judge said: "With that we will adjourn for the day. All lawyers meet in my office tomorrow morning at 8:00 a.m. The jurors report to the courtroom no later than 9:00 a.m.

CHAPTER 27

The next morning at 8:00 all the lawyers were in the judge's chambers for their morning meeting. The judge asked: "When will you put the defendant on the stand?"

They said: "Either today or tomorrow."

The judge asked: "How many more witnesses?"

Harry said; "Maybe 3 more wouldn't you say Isaac?"

Isaac said: "I would agree to that."

At 9:00 everybody entered the courtroom and the bailiff called everyone to order. He yelled: "ALL RISE!!!" Everyone rose and the judge said: "You may be seated. Good morning jurors. This case is nearing the end. I promise it won't be too much longer. Harry, call your next withness please."

Harry said: "I call John Reyes to the stand." As John approached he was sworn in as the next witness. Then he took the stand.

Harry asked: "How long have you known the defendant?"

John said; "I don't really know him at all. I was there at his arrest."

Harry asked: "Was he cooperative in his being arrested?"

John said: "Yes. He was very cooperative. He just stood there stunned like a deer in the headlights. We had no problem getting the handcuffs on him."

Harry asked: "Did he make a statement at the time of his arrest?"

John said: "Yes sir. He said he would do anything to get out of this. Of course every perpetrator who gets arrested says that. But this time he really meant it. He answered every question we could throw at him. He gave us his partner's name and address. We went out and arrested him too."

Harry asked: Were you there when the bomb went off?"

John said: "No sir. That was a whole different squad. I was filled in on the details in the morning."

Harry asked: "What can you tell us about the fight he had?"

John said: "I am not aware of any fight. Whatever

he did to whomever did not happen in front of me. I was not privy to it."

Harry said: "Thank you John. No more questions your honor."

The judge said: "Very well. Isaac, do you have any questions for this witness?"

Isaac said: "Yes your honor. Now John, aren't you involved with the bomb squad?"

John said: "No sir. I am involved with the mounted police. That is a whole different unit."

Isaac asked: "Can you diffuse a bomb?"

John said; "I wouldn't get near a bomb with a ten foot pole."

Isaac asked; "Wasn't it your testimony at the oterh trial that you were there?"

John said: "I was there afterwards. I was there to interview people who were there. The question you asked me was if I was there."

Isaac asked: "What was your role in being there?"

John said: "I just said why I was there. I was there to interiew people. You should listen a little more carefully." With that there were snickers from around the courtroom.

The judge interrupted and said: "That will be enough of that John. Knock off the wisecracks."

John said: "I apologize your honor. I didn't mean any disrespect intended."

The jduge said: "You may step down John. Harry, call your next witness please."

Harry said: "I call Peter O'Donnell to the stand." As Peter arrpached he was sworn in as the next witness.

Harry asked: "Peter, how are you involved in this case?"

Peter said: "I was shocked when I learned that I had to testify. I have never done this before."

The judge said: "Peter, just relax and answer the questions as best you can. Don't worry about the outcome of the trial."

Peter said: "Okay your honor."

Harry asked: "How long have you been a train conductor?"

Peter said: "I have been a train conductor for five years now."

Harry asked: "Have you ever had any incidents on your train?"

Peter said: "Occassionally we have fights, but they don't really last too long. Just drunks who don't know what they are doing. We throw them off the train and be on our merry way. Nothing of this caliber."

Harry asked: "Nothing this major huh?"

Peter said: "No sir. Nothing like this."

Harry asked: "Have you been working since the incident?"

Peter said: "No sir. I have been on disability ever since. I can't even look at a train anymore. I keep seeing the aftermath of the incident."

Harry asked: "Were there any fatalities in this bombing?"

Peter said: "I don't know. I guesss I am still in shock."

Harry asked: "Is this permanent disability?"

Peter said: "I don't know yet. I am just taking it one day at a time."

Harry asked: "What happened the day of the incident?"

Peter said: "Between the Venetian and the Imperial stops somebody pulled the emergency cord. Everybody went flying. I had to get out and walk the length of the track. When I got back there were the hostage takers and 3 adults and a baby. I was ordered into the next car. I called the dispatcher from my cell phone. Then I heard the cops coming."

Harry asked: "What did you do in the next car?"

Peter said: "I tried to piece it all together what was

happening. I kept everybody calm and they followed my lead. Then it dawned on me that nobody was watching us. I told the cops that they were probably amateur hostage takers."

Harry asked: "Did they buy it?"

Peter said: "They seemed to."

Harry said: "Thank you Peter. No more questions your honor."

The judge said: "Isaac, do you have any questions for this witness?"

Isaac said; "Yes your honor. Peter, do you always work such a long shift?"

Peter said: "I was asked to work a double shift that day because someone called in sick."

Isaac asked: "What happened at the bombing?"

Peter said; "I was driving the train and all of a sudden it went BOOM!!!"

Isaac asked; "Was there a crowd on the subway?"

Peter said: "Not at 3:00 in the morning."

Isaac asked: "Were you allowed to eat dinner and lunch during that double shift?"

Peter said: "Yes sir. I got an hour for lunch and an hour for dinner."

Isaac said: "No more questions your honor."

The jduge said: "You may step down Peter. Thank you for your testimony."

With that he left the courthouse. He looked at it as something he can tell his children about and he can write about it in his journal. He started to relax outside the courthouse.

When he thought about it it wasn't so bad after all.

CHAPTER 28

D ay five of the trial started with Marvin. The lawyers gathered in the courtroom and started the day. The judge said: "Harry, you may call your first witness."

Harry said: "I call Marvin to the stand." As Marvin approached the stand he was sworn in as a witness. Harry asked: "Marvin, how long have you been a cop?"

Marvin said: "I have been a cop for fifteen years now."

Harry asked: "Have you ever been injured in the line of duty?"

Marvin said: "No sir. I have been lucky in that regard."

Harry asked: "What happened the day of the incident?"

Marvin said: "I was appointed as the hostage negotiator. My job is to end a hostage situation peacefully without injury."

Harry asked: "Did you deal with the defendant?"

Marvin said: "No sir. I dealt with his partner more."

Harry asked: "What were his original charges?"

Marvin said: "He was charged with planting the bomb."

Harry said: "No more questions your honor."

The judge said: "Yes your honor. Marvin, what did the defendant say to you?"

Marvin said: "Nothing at all."

Isaac asked: "Didn't you interview him?"

Marvin said: "No sir. I was not there after his arrest."

Isaac said; "No more questions your honor."

The judge said: "Very well. You may step down Marvin. We will now break for lunch." With that everybody left and went to eat. They all returned an hour later for the afternoon session.

CHAPTER 29

When they all returned feeling refreshed the judge said: "Harry, please call your next witness."

Harry said; "I call Norman to the stand." As Normal approached he was sworn in as the next witness.

Harry asked; "Norma, what is your involvement in this case?"

Norman said: "I am the chief of police. I was in a meeting with Robert when his cell phone rang off. He said it was his wife. I know his wife and she knows enough not to disturb Robert during a meeting. She has never broken that rule. I told him to answer it."

Harry asked: "What was your reaction to the news of the situation?"

Normal said: "I was mortified that somebody would harm any of them. I treat all my men and their families like they are family. I stopped the meeting to calm down Robert and to redirect his focus."

Harry asked: How did you accomplish this?"

Norman said: "Another officer took hhim into the next office and go over the old case files."

Harry asked: What was this meeting about?"

Norman said: "I don't even remember anymore. Maybe Robert remembers. It will come back to me when it is ready."

Harry said: "No more questions your honor."

The judge asked: "Isaac, do you have any questions for this witness?"

Isaac said: "Yes your honor. Norman, what did you do for Robert personally during this crisis, not speaking professionally."

Norman said: "Around 6:00 that evening I went to the trouble of going to Robert's house and walking his dog. He came home from the hospital just when I was returning. I spent the night at his house. I gave him the next day off so he can go to the hospital and discharge his wife. He was surprised I thought about the dog. He was so distracted all day that he forgot all about her."

Isaac said: "No more questions your honor."

The judge said: "Very well. You may step down Norman. We are finished for the day. Tomorrow we will hear from the defendant himself and then closing arguments. Have a nice evening everybody. With that the bailiff yelled: "ALL RISE!!!"

Everybody left the courthouse.

CHAPTER 30

The next day everybody was excited to close the case. The jduge entered and actually smiled. He only smiled on the days when the cases came to a close. The lawyeres thought his face was going to crack into two pieces. The judge said: "Good morning everyone. Harry, call your next witness please."

Harry said: "I call Aaron Abramovitch to the stand." As Aaron approached he was sworn in as the next witness.

Harry asked: "How did you get involved in this case?"

Aaron said: "My partner in crime was my cell mate in jail. We got out and hung out together."

Harry asked: "Are you still on parole?"

Aaron said: "Yes. I finish in about 4 years."

Harry asked: "What provoked you to do this?"

Aaron said: "My partner has a hold on me that I can't resist. When he says jump I leap."

Hary asked: "What was your role in this scenario?"

Aaron said: "I was supposed to plant the bomb that went off. I set the timer wrong for 3:00 a.m. instead of 3:00 p.m. Abrham wanted to shoot me himself he was so mad because I screwed up."

Harry asked: "Have you ever handled a bomb before:"

Aaron said: "No sir. I really didn't know what I was doing. When we were in the train I was so scared that I felt heart palpitations. I was sweating bullets. I couldn't even hold the gun steady."

Harry asked: "Why did you and Abraham cook up this scheme?"

Aaron said: "Abraham and I applied for an engineer's job but was rejected. We stood in line for six hours and got nowhere. Abraham took it personally."

Harry asked: "Why were you rejected?"

Aaron said: "We didn't have an engineer's license. I didn't know you needed one."

Harry said: "No more questions your honor."

The judge said: "Isaac, do you have any questions for this witness?"

Isaac said: "Yes sir. I do."

Isaac asked: "Aaron, why didn't you just say no to Abraham?"

Aaron said; "You just don't say no to Abraham."

Isaac asked: "Why did you stay in touch with Abraham after he was released?"

Aaron said: "I didn't know anybody here in Las Vegas. I am not allowed to leave the state until my probation expires. I would talk to the squirrel if he gives me an audience. Sometimes I feel like The Ignored, a book I read. People pass me right by without even noticing me. Do you know how it feels to be invisible? Trust me. It is the lonliest feeling in the world."

Isaac asked: "Doesn't anybody ever talk to you?"

Aaron said: "Once in a while. I am usually approached by a beggar looking for change."

Isaac asked: "Why don't you join a church or something?"

Aaron said: "I was ignored as a stranger even in Temple. I am Jewish. Still I was a part of the wall. I just blend in with the furniture."

Isaac said: "No more questions your honor."

The judge said: "Very well. You may step down Aaron."

With that he returned to his seat at the defense table.

CHAPTER 31

The jduge addressed the jury and said: "Ladies and gentleme. After lunch we will hear closing arguments from the lawyers. You will then adjourn to the room and start deliberations.

After lunch everybody returned right on time. The judge said: "Ladies and gentlemen. You have heard both sides of the argument. How long the deliberations take is entirely up to you. It makes no different to me how long you take. Harry, please begin when read."

Harry got up and said: "Ladies and gentlemen of the jury. I believe I have proven that Aaron did this heinous act. I believe he admitted that he planted that bomb. Please fin this defendant guilty of planting the bomb."

The jduge said; "Isaac, you may begin your closing arguments."

Isaac said: "You have heard why my client is guilty. He couldn't even hold the gun steady.

He never handled the bomb correctly and didn't know what he was doing. All my client is guilty of is wanting to be noticed and wanting a friend. If anything society is to blame for not guiding him to make better choices and to have better options offered to him. Just picture yourselves being ignored day in and day out. You will know what my client is going through. Thank you."

CHAPTER 32

The jurors were brought into the deliberations room to begin. They entered to a surprise from the judge. They had coffee, juice, milk, cups, and cookies and fruit. After about a half hour they started to get down the business at hand. Juror number six said: "I personally don't buy into this scheme that nobody noticed him. I have been feeling like that all my life and I didn't plant any bombs. I am just skating through life trying to eek out a living. Nobody said life was easy. That doesn't give you the right to injure other people."

Juror number seven said: "Wait a second my friend. You seem to forget that nobody was injured. Everybody thought it was thunder."

Juror number four said: "You forget. There was one fatality. May we call for a read back?"

They were told to write a note and the bailiff will get it for them. The bailiff came back 10 minutes later with the read back that said there was one fatality.

Juror number seven said: "I stand corrected. You are right. There was one fatality."

This was a lively debate that satisfied all of them. Then the vote came. It took only one vote to come to a unanimous decision to declare the defendant guilty of planting the bomb. They took time to giggle at the closing arguments that society was to blame for him doing this heinous act. When they returned to court juror number one was the spokesman. The judge said: "Has the jury reached a verdict?"

The juror said: "We have your honor."

The judge said: "Will the defendant please rise?"

The defendant rose and the judge said: "What is your verdict?"

The juror said: "We find the defendant guilty!!!"

The judge said: "Ladies and gentlemen of the jury. Thank you for your service. You are now excused."

When they all left the judge said: "As for you young man. You will return to the jail and serve out the rest of your four years back in jail. Bailiffs, remove this defendant in handcuffs and put him in a holding cell until such time as he is picked up and transported. Good day everybody."

THE END

Here are excepts from my next novel coming out hopefully this year. I am going to marry off John. The title will be John's Wedding. What happens at the wedding will make you fall off your chair. It will be most enjoyable. This is the start of it. Naturally with this gang something goes awry. Stay tuned to see what happens.

John's Wedding

By Wendy Elmer

Chapter 1

May 27th was the start of the Memorial Day weekend. The crowds in Las Vegas were starting to build up and the whole city, strip, and police department was gearing up for the busy days ahead. Everybody on the strip squad was prepared to come to work with a smile and a friendly hello to the visitors. John was working his usual part time shift at the Motel 6 in the beginning of the strip. He met the most beautiful woman he ever saw. She said she had no reservations anywhere, but wanted to come to Las Vegas on the spur of the moment. She was hoping for a room somewhere. John's mouth went dry as a bone and his tongue turned white because of no saliva. All he could do was to stare at the woman. He thought he was looking at an angel from heaven. She asked for a room. The manager came over and had to slap him in the back of the head to wake him up. All he had to do was to answer the woman's question.

The manager said: "Please forgive his rudeness. He doesn't mean to stare. He can give you room 12. Have you ever been here before?"

The woman said: "No sir. I just wanted to check it out for the weekend."

The manager said: "John, please take the woman's luggage to room 12. If you need anything madam please pick up the phone and call the front desk. He will regain the power of speech by the time he returns to the office. Go John."

John said: "Yes sir. Please forgive me for staring. You are just the most interesting person I have met since I have been here. I am also a cop during the week when I am not working here. If you need anything madam please just call the front desk."

The woman said: "Thank you John. Please direct me to the nearest place to eat."

John said: "That would be the Burger King right down the road. About 3 stores down."

After a nap she felt like she was ready to eat. Then she went out and brought it back to the room.

Chapter 2

On Tuesday of that next week John returned to work at the police station. He almost busted down the door running into Robert's office. He interrupted a meeting Robert was having with Norman. Robert got so scared he dropped his coffee cup in his lap again.

Robert said: "Holy Tarnation John. What has gotten you all hiped up?"

John said: "I AM IN LOVE!! I AM GETTING MARRIED!!!"

Norman said: "Congratulations John. What is the name of the lucky girl?"

John said: "I can't remember right now. I think she said her name was Michelle or something like that."

Norman asked: "When is the lucky date?

John said: "Christmas Eve. December 24th of this year."

Robert said: "Will this be a small wedding or a big extravagant affair?""

John said: "I think we are going to have a big wedding."

Norman said: "You have to start looking for a place now. Most places are booked up a year in advance for a reception. Do you have a place to get married?"

John said: "Yes sir. We are getting married in St. Peter's church. The church is booked up. It will be an afternoon wedding because my fiance said she is not a night person. She prefers to do things first thing in the morning. The Mass will start at 1:00 in the afternoon. It will be a high Mass with incense and the whole shebang. It reminds her of her childhood Masses. She is from Colorado originally. She comes from a religious family. We have so much in common. Maybe we are brother and sister."

Robert said: "God I hope not. That would be illegal to marry a sibling in this state or any state for that matter.

John asked: "Is it really possible to have so much in common with someone you just met?"

Robert said: "Yes. But you should wait for the other shoe to drop. I think you should get to know this person better before you marry. Take the next six months and when you do your pre-cannon training you will learn about how far in debt she is and whether or not she is a credit card abuse."

Robert said: "Wait a second. As a personal favor to you I can do a background check on this person to see if she is all that."

John asked: "All that what?"

Robert said: "It is just an expression John. It means is she really what she seems to be?"

John said: "Oh okay Robert. See what you can dig up for me. By the way. Would you two and Ronald be my best men?"

Robert said: "I would be more than thrilled to be your best man. Ronald and Norman would be considered your groomsmen. I will call Ronald and find out if he is up to it."

Normally you would have a lady going down on the arm of the groomsmen. That means that you would need 2 ladies. I can use my wife Joyce. Ronald can use his wife Eloise and Norman can use his wife Nancy."

John said: "Perfect!! Then that is all settled. What do we do next?"

Robert said: "Find time to buy the wedding rings. You need one for you and one for your wife."

John said: "I think I need to go to the bathroom I am so excited."

Norman said "Go John. Don't come back for at least 15 minutes and when you do you will open that door like the mature adult I know is inside you somewhere."

With that he exited the room nicely.

Norman said: "What are we going to do with that child?"

Robert said: "Don't worry about him. He is just a man in love. I am sure you walked into walls and did crazy things before you got married. Just keep an eye on him and make sure he doesn't fall off a building or fall down the stairs. I have to make sure his work doesn't suffer. I have to keep him focused on his job. Luckily we are between cases right now."

Norman said: "I will get started on the background check. You get on the horn with Eloise and ask Ronald if he will do this for us."

Robert picked up the phone and dialed Ronald's number. He answered on the first ring. He was overjoyed about being asked to be part of a wedding. He accepted for himself and Eloise before he can finish the sentence. Eloise started screaming in excitement. Ronald told Robert that he will help

John in any way he can. He is looking forward to it. What about out daughter Arlene?"

Robert said: "For now let us say we can bring her with us. She will be no trouble at all."

Norman returned with the finished product of the background check. He said she was clean as a whistle. No arrests, no drug busts, not even a driver's license. Her credit check came back in excellent standing. Norman gave this woman his blessing for this marriage. Father Raaser came up with a special idea for this wedding. That will be revealed shortly.

Thank you to all my faithful readers. You will not be disappointed with this book. I love weddings.

ABOUT THE AUTHOR

I have been writing for a few years now. This is my 6th novel. I live in the city of New York and I work in a library. Some minor characters are introduced into this novel as well as the next one. The 7th novel is already in the writing stages.

I have been writing for a few years now. This is my 6th novel. I live in the city of New York and I work in a library. Some minor characters are introduced into this novel as well as the next one. The 7th novel is already in the writing stages.